CW00865715

Please,
Speak with me Earthly..,

- Kardhajannat, my lovely daughter what are you looking on your room window? Alyssa said
- I simply try to remember Mama. I try to stay alone.
_ What do you like to remember when you are alone?
_ I try fasting listening any music. My ears became sick.
_ What do you mean my heart?
_ No one loves me Mama.
- Really do you think that my lovely daughter? Don't worry you are not a girl for sale you are lady who takes her time to think before deciding any thing.
- it is very hard mama to know the reality. I do not like to know any more.
-No matter to stress your self.

Kardhajannat cover your room window with your old window textile you are not obliged to update by your room light what is in your mind. Come my lovely daughter to the kitchen to prepare some thing to eat for all the family.

- What my grand father bought for today.

- We have bio Gelbe Carrots and onion, we could mixe it with paprika sauce for making Sirene salad the Tunisian traditional "Slatet Houriyya"

-My colleagues in the past in the primary schooll never believe that I could eat Paprika sauce when they look to my face as a white girl with black eyes they imagine that I am very sensitive never I could eat paprika Sauce.

- Do not stress our self by that Kardhajannet, we will never paint the door of our apartment as red color to update with food times it is not our business. it is not our family time.

-Since I have my monthly period mama I became discovering lot of ironies from my colleagues. I have really no idea why?

-May be because You do not consommate yet the 28 days period tablet . it is not your business.

- When this tablet was created mama?

- I suppose that it was invented since the Turkish were planning to manage slavery sales of women in Tunis since 1928 with the cooperation of old French jealousy architecture planning in Tunis around

the Traditional Madina In Tunis.
No matter to discover their chains
since they are born in Tunis.
-It is really absurd Mama.
- Please my daughter come and help
me in the kitchen.
-Could I know Mama, why did my
grand parents chose the first floor to
live in their private apartment in El
Mourouj 1?
-It is simply for wishing good luck for
the future married girls of our family
when They become married. Our girls
are not for sale.
-Why my father Steffen did not come
back to us Mama. Could I know the
reason please?
-I have no Idea Kardhajannet till now
we did not leave the place where we
were together before deciding to

have a baby. I mean you.
- My coleagues since primary school look at me with irony when their parents meet them after courses inside their cars with their fathers and mothers and concerning me me only you you come walking to me alone without my father. I feel my self very poor mama.
-You are not poor My Kardhajannet. you should never be annoyed by this absurdity.
I showed to you the picture of your father before he went to Europe after the call of his father by phone to inform him that lot of dangerous thing could be happen in Germany. No matter to know more my Khardhajannet you are not for sale.

- some colleagues when I showed to them the picture of my father told me that they don't believe that he is my father. They think that he left you because you are an easy woman and he is not proud of me as his daughter. I feel myself very poor mama.

-really is it that what do they told you and think. It is really stupid, they are only jealous because you are not yet a computer program in the room in the apartment of your grand parents. This apartment is not for slavery sales. these colleagues are only jealous my lovely daughter. never be annoyed by them. it is only absurd.

-So mama what could be the solution when they tell me nearly daily that

I do not look like the face of my father?

- My Kardhajannet do you like to visit the oldest Zawya in Monastir where was the grave of a Saint Man who spent all his life traying to resolve the disputation between traditional families in the poorest village in Monastir since many centuries and not looking to earn any money when it is resolved.

- What do you mean Mama, do you because believing of magical phenomenology.

It is better my daughter than spending all your life discussing absurdity with jealous people. Till now I am proud of you and no one can change this. It is like eternal believe my lovely daughter.

. What is the name of this Zawya Mama in Monastir?

-it is "Sidi El Mayel" Zawya build since Viking time in Monastir beach, when the beach was just on the oldest farms of many generations of my family. Actually the sea is not any more on the oldest farms of my family. this parts of sea became a very salty ground not you could plant their as a farm. You could if you like visit the patrimoine "Uzita" Mozaics made since the vikings and Vandals where they where living in the past in Monastir village when the sea was just on the farms of my family.

- Could you tell me Mama what the people do in this "Sidi El Mayed Zawya" in Monastir?

-Mostly the young generations there

ask simple question, could they be lucky if they are planning to be married with other people.

That it could not be braking family ages between if they decide to be married.

- What does it mean Mama, I understand nothing.

- If you would like to understand my Kadhajannet you could read the Tunisian Arabic Adalucian book of the Tunisian Ibn Khaldun to explain to you how to try to chose the right time of married for avoiding braking family ages when you decide to be married with some one.

-What does it mean, the people who visit this poorest Zawya Sidi El Mayed in Monastir were reading the book of the first sociology writer in in History.

Yes my lovely daughter you could be proud of the poor Tunisian Ibn Khaldun. He is an andalucian Astrologue who was living in Tunis in the past with his family and who spent all his life in Turkish Jail when he discovered the system of slavery palnning in Europ of Byzantin empire. You do not need to be addicted to that. It is only Absurd.

I think my lovely daughter, I made you learning the Tunisian arabic language to be able able to read the book of the Tunisian Ibn Khaldun, if my destiney is to dye very early so you could have this old book in your room library to understund the history in your country Tunisia how it was without masks. I have no more

mission to do as your mother.
-So What could be the solution
Mama, when my colleagues makes
mockeries to me that I do not look
like m father.
- You do not need to be a monkey
my Kadhajannet.
-At the right time when you choose
to be married with the right one, just
before one or two years I will promise
your your face will be like your father
face shape as this old picture of your
father. You are not obliged to be a
computer trying to convince your
stupid colleagues about. They have
only a lavage de Cerveau. if they like
to make copy Past to you face and
after they make revenge. You don't
need them if this is their only
ambition with you.

-So tell me Mama how could I be sure that I could be like having the same face shape of my father when I become older?

- First of all choose the right husband which you dream of not whom which you would like to earn from it is not the business of our traditional family in Tunisia.

-So After, tell me please.

-After Khardhajannet take your time to know your future husband, you are an not an instant machine of marriage, it is not our business and the intermediate who make this business we don't need them they are only hypocrite people who try to have some tips of marriage giving the illusion to insure the future marriage. Also we do not need them.

-Please mama tell me how could my face before marriage becomes like the old shape face of my father naturally? Tell me Please.

- I will give you a bio recipe from he oldest Sidi El Mayel Zawya that could insure you that your birth name is not a fake and that you could be proud of the both birth names of your mother and the birth name of your father before the contract of marriage with your future husband. The traditional marriage contract in Tunisia is a quadra family names insurance not only one birth name of the husband. For that reason you should choose the right time of marriage it is not a game.

- Tell me please Mama, how could my face look like the old face shape of my father naturally when I decide to be married.

-First of all, you should never forget to be proud of the birth name of your mother and the birth name of your father althought lot of colleagues makes mockeries to your birth names. It is not their business and if no one has the intention to be married with you so no matter to be engaged with them.

-Tell me Mama Please how could my face becomes naturally looking like the shape face of my father, please Mama, please Answer me.

-Kiss your mother first like you was doing all time when you was a kid I do not like that you become having illusion about any think I told you about since you was a kid. I have no ambition to lie it is not my objective

to have a tip of lying.
- Tell me Please, please, please
Mama, how could my face looks
naturally like the shape face of my
father when he was young?
-Come to the bathroom my
Kadhajanned I will teach you the
Astrology as you wish and without
you pay any tip for that it is not my
business.
-Ok, what could you do to me, what
was you doing to me as a baby ha ha
ha.
-Don't worry ya Kardha, I will not sell
you in any food shop as a baby,
come my stupid girl.
First of all wear a tshirt and your
cyclist shirt which you was wearing
during you became swimming in the
beach with a cyclist shirt when you

became adolescent not more swimming with Bikini as a kid.

-Ok Mama I do we go now to the bathroom.

-Stay in the Bathroom Kadhajanned till I bring from the Kitchen the oldest bio recipe to check how could your face becomes naturally looking like the face shape of your father. I am coming, wait do not go out.

-What did you bring mama What is that?

-It is Bio Butter, Sesame Oil, Cumin, and this is an old Alpen salt saved since many generations in the kitchen of my grand grand parents. In the poorest village in Monastir where is the Zawya Sidi El Mayed.

-Ok, and after what are you planning with that with me?

- Your soft hair Kardhajanned needs to be voluminous it has not enough minerals, I will tell you how naturally you could add minerals to you hair for discovery your beauty first after for being sure that your face could look like the face shape of your father.

Go to the kitchen first and bring the kitchen paper to use for your hair during drying this bio recipe on your hair.

My lovely Daughter these plastic gloves I use during mixing this recipe on your hair which is without any artificial coloration.

-Ok And After, you look being mama professional concerning knowing the natural hair coloration. haha it is funny.

My stupid girl, you do not run for coloring your hair in any barber shop with artificial coloration we do not need their punctual artificial colors it is not our business, we simply take our time till our hair becomes beautiful naturally.

-It looks interesting thing Mama. Please start to cure the minerals of my hair, it is very soft.

-Very good, perfect, I cover now your hair with kitchen paper to be enough warm in Winter time, I will give you my old cushion which I was using when I was a kid in the past in the home my parent during I use this recipe on my hair for having a traditional natural healthy hair without any chemical composition of any actual barber shop.

-How long time time should I have this bio hair mask on my hair Mama?
-You spend a night with till your hair absorb perfectly the different minerals.
-Mama, Mama, wake up please, wake up, I feel having so much blood pressure in brain. What does it mean?
-It is normal Khardhajannet, it is a fortified nutritionl minerals to your neurons activated quickly with healthy mineral do no worry if you have some asymetric face.
-What, what does it mean Mama.
-I think my daughter why you hait nearly daily the bad words of your colleagues making mockeries about your birth name you could have a brain stroke since you are kids when try to speak at first time. Do not

Do not worry my daughter , you detserny is not being handicap when stay proud of your birth name.
-Please, what was you doing to me Mama. Was you never telling me That I was born As handicap. No, No No...
-Do not be scared please my daughter no one will make mockeries to you as handicap baby as some colleagues when they are in your classroom in primary school when you chose the first table to sit in , when they make mockeries to you as saying" The priorities is to the handicap people" You do not need to speak with these people Kardhajannet , they are only having "Lavage de Cerveau".

My Lovely daugther tell where do you feel the asymetry bones in your body we resolve that just after one week my Kardhajannet naturally. without being scanned in any doctor laboratory who desire to sell your bones.

-Are you meaning Mama, that since I was a kid I had a brain stroke when I tryed to speak.

-May be Kardhajannet, Tell me My daughter where do you feel the Asymetry.

-Here, Here, here..., I feel that the half of my body in bigger that the other half of my body. What could be the solution tell me please, tell me , tell me please Mama.

-The solution is very simple my daughter not complicated, I mix for you Butter and Alpen Salt, you do massage to the shortest part of bones in your asymetric body and face, when you feel that the bones becomes nearly symetric complete the massage to the complete body that your bones could grow up symetrically and naturally till now you are not a computer of 28 days of monthly period we do not need this system of Turkish logiciel in our apartment, you are not any bone in your room as symbolic architecture, it is not our business.we do not need to sell your bones to any Byzantine Turkish.

-Mama, My face looks nearly symetric now, should I continue to add the Alpen salt and butter to my complete face or not.Or Is it makeup?

Lightning Source UK Ltd.
Milton Keynes UK
UKHW012028300720
367452UK00005BA/148

9 781715 225520